Now, *that's* what I call Christmas spirit.

Not!

I had been looking forward to making some crank phone calls this evening. But after this disgusting display of cheerfulness, crank phone calls were not going to be enough. This year, the Whos were going to get more . . . much more. I'd tie up the entire phone system before I was through!

I was going to figure out a way to ruin Christmas in Whoville if it was the last thing I did.

Adapted by Louise Gikow

Based on the motion picture screenplay
written by
Jeffrey Price & Peter S. Seaman

Based on the book by Dr. Seuss

RANDOM HOUSE NEW YORK

 Published in the United States by Random House, Inc.,
New York, and simultaneously in Canada by Random House of
Canada Limited, Toronto.

www.randomhouse.com/seussville www.universalstudios.com

Library of Congress Cataloging-in-Publication Data
Gikow, Louise.
Dr. Seuss' How the Grinch stole Christmas / adapted by Louise Gikow.
p. cm. — "Based on the motion picture screenplay written by Jeffrey
Price ... [et al.] ; based on the book by Dr. Seuss."
SUMMARY: A retelling, based on the film version, in which the Grinch
tries to stop Christmas from arriving in Whoville by stealing all the
presents and food.
ISBN 0-375-81062-5
[1. Christmas—Fiction.] I. Seuss, Dr. How the Grinch stole Christmas.
II. How the Grinch stole Christmas (Motion picture : 2000). III. Title.
PZ7.G369 Dr 2000 [E]—dc21 00-041739

Printed in the United States of America October 2000

10 9 8 7 6 5 4

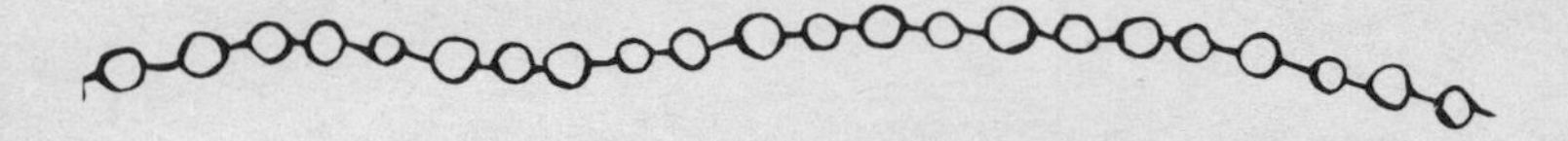

Dr. Seuss'
HOW THE
GRINCH
STOLE
CHRISTMAS!

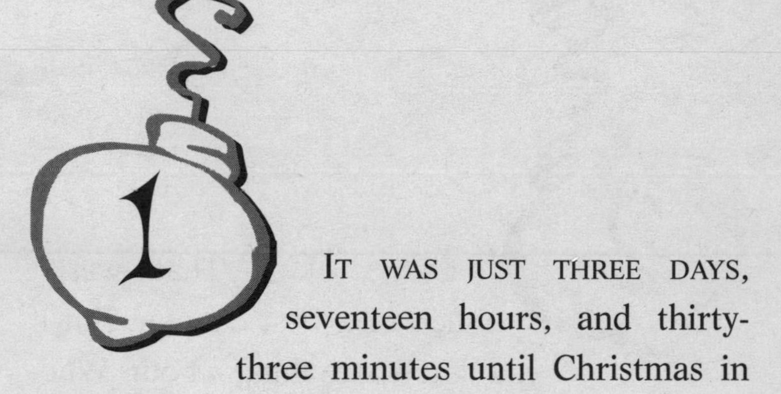

It was just three days, seventeen hours, and thirty-three minutes until Christmas in Whoville.

2

OKAY, OKAY. That wasn't much of a first chapter. But if you know anything about Whoville—and I have to assume you do, due to an extremely famous and totally odious book that I'm sure your parents read to you when you were a tiny child—you know what Christmas in Whoville is all about. I didn't think I had to go into all the disgusting details . . .

I do? Oh. Well. In that case . . .

First of all, it was snowing. It *always*

snows just before Christmas in Whoville. You know the song "I'm Dreaming of a White Christmas . . . (just like the ones I used to know)"? Well, Christmas in Whoville is just like the ones you used to know. In fact, it's *better* than the ones you used to know.

For one thing, there's the snow itself. We're not talking just any old snow here. This snow comes packaged in perfect, fat white flakes that float lightly through the sky, covering everything with a soft layer that is the perfect depth for snowball fights and sleigh rides and sledding down hills. And what's even worse, the snow in Whoville never, *ever* turns into that yellowy sludge like it always does where *you* live. It remains pure, pristine . . . yeah, that's right, perfect.

For another, there's the tree. The tree in the Whoville town square is the biggest, most beautiful tree you've ever seen. Perfect size, shape, color—the Whoville tree even *smells* perfect. It's decorated with perfectly shiny, perfectly colored ornaments, at least a ton of silvery tinsel, and more multicolored lights than you can count in . . . in . . . three days, seventeen hours, and thirty-three minutes.

Which, incidentally, is all the time the Whos have left in which to count them . . .

But I'm getting ahead of myself.

On this particularly perfect third-day-before-Christmas, the Whos were indulging in their favorite pastime of the Christmas season—Christmas shopping.

"Come on, Cindy Lou!" Lou Lou Who cried as he pulled his six-year-old daughter through the crowd of Whos who had already filled the streets of the main square. "We've got to keep shop-shop-shopping! Oh, my. Look at the time . . ."

Stu and Drew Lou Who—Cindy Lou's older brothers—dashed past, late for school again.

"Hey, Dad!" shouted Stu.

"Hey, boys! Have a good day at school!" Lou shouted back cheerily.

"Whatever," said Drew.

Lou barreled on, Cindy Lou in tow. "Yep. Early in the morning. Best time to shop. This way, we beat the rush!" Lou gave his daughter a big, cheerful grin as a tall Who rushed past, stepping hard on Cindy Lou's foot. The tall Who rammed into a short Who, who was rushing the other way.

"I'm telling you, Cindy Lou, this is my favorite day of the year . . . three days before Christmas," Lou went on. "Heads up!"

Two Whos rushed past on a bicycle, too focused on their argument to notice that they had almost run over Cindy Lou.

"Home to bake!"

"Out to shop!"

"Home to shop!!!"

"Out to bake!!!"

"Then, of course," Lou went on, ignoring

the quarrel, "there's two days before Christmas . . . and Christmas Eve, what with the Whobilation and all. Duck!"

Lou and Cindy Lou ducked under a Who carrying a gigantic stack of packages.

"And then, of course, there's Christmas itself." Lou nodded. "That's gotta be up there on *any* list."

Lou let go of Cindy Lou's hand for a moment. She was immediately swept off into the bustling crowd.

"Daddy!" Cindy Lou cried.

Lou looked up, noticed that his daughter was receding from view, and held up his hand. Cindy Lou found herself being passed back to him by a hundred helpful Whos.

"Then again, there's the day *after* Christmas."

Cindy Lou reached her father and was set gently at his feet. Lou smiled down at her. "You know what? They're *all* great! Come on!" He grabbed Cindy Lou's hand and they headed back into the fray.

Yes, that's Christmas in Whoville. Full of cheerful Whos just filled to overflowing with the holiday spirit of giving and getting . . .

Bah, humbug.

YOU PROBABLY GUESSED IT by now.

I am the Grinch.

Well, if somebody had to tell this story, I figured it might as well be me. At least you'll get the truth.

And, of course, they're paying me a bundle. After all, I am somewhat of a celebrity.

So, here are my back-of-the-jacket vital statistics: I live in a cave on Mt. Crumpit, just north of Whoville. It's a delightful place—

damp, moldy, chilly, and thoroughly unpleasant. The Whos know well enough to leave me alone. Well, not exactly alone—I share my miserable domicile with Max. He's a dog. But don't worry—he's not one of those teensy-weensy, cutesy-wootsie, itty-bitty dogs. Nor is he a big, furry, friendly, shaggy, waggy dog. He's a scraggly, grumpy, no-good mutt. After all, I have my reputation to think of.

Now, where was I? Oh, yes.

As I was saying before I so rudely interrupted myself, usually the Whos leave me alone.

But on this *particular* day, four teenage Whos were climbing up Mt. Crumpit in the direction of my cave.

Now, *that* was foolish of them.

The two Who boys were Stu and Drew Lou Who, whom you met in the last chapter. (Too bad for you!) They were desperately trying to impress two Who girls who were with them.

"I thought you said there was some amazing mistletoe up here," I overheard Junie Who say. Of course, I was monitoring them through my Grinchy periscope.

"It's all near the top," Drew told her. "C'mon."

That was a mistake.

Junie frowned. "The top? We're not supposed to—"

Christina Who interrupted her. "Just humor them," she whispered. "They're kinda cute."

Cute? A teenage Who? I don't *think* so.

"Hey, Stu!" Drew shouted in what must have been his "impress the girls" voice. "I'll bet I can beat you to that rock."

"Naw," Stu replied. "I can beat *you!*"

"You're on!" Drew answered. "Go!"

And the two boys dashed off for the top of Mt. Crumpit. MY Mt. Crumpit.

It wasn't very smart of them. Four Whos, one Grinch? I'll take those odds any day.

By now, Junie was realizing that climbing

past the Old Whoville Dump toward the top of Mt. Crumpit was perhaps not the most intelligent way to spend a pre-Christmas day . . . or any other day, for that matter, if you happen to be a Who.

"Where are we?" she asked nervously, looking around. "I think we should go back."

Stu laughed.

"Why?" he asked. "Don't tell me you're afraid of the Grinch!"

"Uh . . . no . . . ," said Junie.

That was a mistake.

"They say he lives up here in a cave, and he only comes out when he's hungry for the taste of Who flesh," Drew proclaimed dramatically.

Who flesh, indeed! They flatter themselves. The thought of eating Who flesh makes my stomach crawl. I'd rather chew on dead maggots. No, really—they're quite tasty when sautéed in a little motor oil . . .

Suddenly, there was a rustling sound.

"What was *that?*" Christina looked worried.

"Now it's over there!" Stu's voice sounded a little shaky. He peered around . . . and then he heard it again, the same ominous rustling sound. And . . . there! Weren't the leaves in that bush shaking just a bit? "There's something in the bushes!" he gasped.

Duh.

"Grinch!" shouted Drew. And, leaving the girls to fend for themselves, he and Stu ran off.

Typical male Who behavior.

Christina and Junie, rooted to the spot, watched the bushes in horror. The leaves rustled again . . . and . . . and . . . a tiny brown squirrel hopped out, sniffed the air, and scurried up a tree.

"Ha!" Junie said weakly. "I *knew* there was no such thing as the Grinch." And she and Christina started to laugh.

No such thing as the Grinch?

Well, you and I know better, don't we?

You and I also know that old saying, don't

we? The one that goes, "He who laughs last, laughs best"? Or in this case, would it be *she?*

Well, I can assure you that the last one to laugh in this neck of the woods is always me.

4

WHEN CHRISTINA AND JUNIE caught up with Stu and Drew, the two boys were farther up the mountain, breathing hard and looking terrified.

"Hey, you silly poopers, you missed it," giggled Christina. "Your Grinch was back there eating some—"

But then she stopped short. Stu and Drew were staring at the door of a big cave. It was overgrown with underbrush and unwelcoming—just like the door to a Grinch's cave should be. It takes a lot of hard work to keep it that way.

"—nuts," Christina finished.

Stu and Drew were already examining the cave door.

"It doesn't look like anyone lives here," said Stu, pushing the door. It opened a little. Stu and Drew peered around the edge of it when—

"RRRRRRRRRRRRRRRRRR!" The door swung open and a gigantic monster with hugc, slavering jaws exploded out of it and went straight for Stu's throat!

"AAAAAAAAAAAAAAAAAH!" screamed the four Who teenagers, racing down the hill for their lives.

Of course, it was only Max—my trusty hound.

"Good boy, Max," I said. "Shall we show them the way down?"

I went back over to my control panel. I paused and then pressed a button labeled TREES.

"We wouldn't want them to *leaf* without fond memories of their visit, now would we, Max?" I laughed as I watched the trees come smashing down around the terrified teens, who were still racing down my mountain, screaming like banshees.

I pushed another button marked LOCUSTS.

The teens were immediately enveloped in a thick swarm of bugs.

"It really *bugs* me when people leave without saying good-bye," I told Max.

Then I tried the button marked SQUALL. Within seconds, hundred-mile-an-hour winds had picked up the four teens and were blowing them all over Mt. Crumpit.

"Today's mountain forecast: partially Grinchy with scattered Whos," I giggled. Sometimes, I really slay me.

Serves 'em right, those yuletide-loving, sickly sweet, nog-sucking cheermongers! I mean, I really don't like 'em. Mm-mm, no, I don't.

And what were Whos doing on my mountain, anyway? They want to get to know me, do they? They want to spend a little *quality* time with the Grinch? Well, I guess I could use a little social interaction . . .

All right, Whoville! If you're hungry for humbug, I'm the special of the day! And I deliver!!!!

5

WHILE THE FOUR WHO teenagers were flying around Mt. Crumpit, the rest of the Who population was . . . oh, take a guess . . . still shopping, did you say?

You . . . are . . . absolutely . . . right!!!!

Lou Lou Who stood on line at Farfingles, the Whoville department store, doing an inventory of all his purchases.

"Let's see," he told Cindy Lou. "We have a snoozlephone for your brother Drew and a snoozlephone for your brother Stu, a muncle for your uncle, a fant for your aunt, and a fandpa for . . . your cousin Leon. Cindy Lou? Cindy Lou?"

Cindy Lou was hidden behind the stack of gifts. She poked her head around it and looked up at her father.

"Dad, doesn't this seem like a bit much?" she asked.

"A bit much? This is what Christmas is all about!" Lou replied enthusiastically, handing the clerk his credit card. "Nothing beats Christmas, does it?"

"I guess," Cindy Lou answered doubtfully.

"You *guess??*" Lou looked at his daughter, astounded.

"Well, it's just that I look around at you and Mom and everyone getting all kerbobbled . . . Doesn't all of this seem . . . superfluous?"

"Yes, yes, it does!" said Lou enthusiastically. Then he stopped short. "*Superfluous* is a good thing, isn't it, Cindy?"

"Uh . . . it means 'unnecessary,'" said Cindy Lou. "Over the top."

"And that's a good thing, right?"

Cindy Lou rolled her eyes.

"Dad!" someone croaked.

Lou looked confused.

"Is your voice changing, Cindy Lou?" he asked his daughter.

"That wasn't me, Dad," Cindy Lou replied.

Lou and Cindy Lou looked around. But all they saw were four rather ugly-looking snow figures.

"Huh?" said Lou.

The four snow figures shook themselves off. They were Drew, Stu, Christina, and Junie.

"What happened to you?" Lou asked, astonished.

The four Who teens huddled together, trembling. Finally, Stu got his chattering teeth to stop chattering long enough so he could speak.

"It was . . . the Grinch!" Stu gasped.

All up and down Main Street, drivers slammed on their brakes, cars squealed to a stop, mouths dropped open, and Whos froze in place, horrified.

As well they should.

"He scared us so bad that Stu cried," Drew said, a little nastily.

"No, Drew cried!" Stu gave Drew a dirty look.

"They *both* cried," said Junie, rolling her eyes.

"What's a Grinch?" Cindy Lou asked, tugging at her father's sleeve.

"Did somebody just say *Grinch?*" a loud voice was suddenly heard to say. And the crowd parted to reveal two solemn-looking Whos—Mayor August May Who and Who Bris, his chief adviser and bootlicker.

"Oh, uh, hello, Mayor May Who, sir," said Lou, groveling just a bit.

Mayor May Who shook his head solemnly.

"Lou, I don't need to remind you," he began, "that this Christmas marks the one thousandth Whobilation . . ."

"Whoville's most important celebration!" Who Bris reminded anyone who needed reminding. Which was nobody.

"And *The Book of Who* says very clearly . . ." Mayor May Who gave Who Bris a dirty look, and Who Bris quickly handed him a dog-eared copy of *The Book of Who*, turned to the appropriate page.

"'Every size of Who we can measure knows that Whobilation is a time we must treasure,'" May Who read. He turned back to Lou. "Now, Lou, please tell me your boys were not up on Mt. Crumpit."

"My boys were not up on Mt. Crumpit," Lou said obediently.

"Although," the mayor proclaimed cheerfully, "we all know that there isn't anyone—or any*thing*—up on Mt. Crumpit, anyway. It's all just a tall tale designed to frighten impressionable schoolchildren." He smiled indulgently at Drew and Stu.

Drew shook his head. "But there *is* a Grinch, Mr. Mayor! We saw him!"

A low, distressed murmur could be heard coming from the crowd.

"You only *think* you saw him," the mayor cut in smoothly.

"No, we did," Drew insisted. "He was big and hairy and—"

"Clearly a figment of your overactive imaginations!" Mayor May Who was beginning to look annoyed. The crowd was getting nervous, and keeping the crowd content and free from any concerns that interfered with Christmas shopping was what kept the mayor in office. "You did *not* see the Grinch. Do you hear?"

"But that's not—" Drew began.

"But he was—" Stu began.

A ripple of panic started through the crowd.

Lou covered Stu's and Drew's mouths with his hands.

"No, no, that's right, Mayor," he said heartily. "The boys didn't see any Grinch. I'm sure they were just up there on the mountain playing with matches, or defacing public property or something—"

The crowd breathed a sigh of relief.

"Good," said Mayor May Who. He looked impatiently around at the gaping crowd. "Well, you heard the man. There's no Grinch problem here. And to celebrate, I hereby decree that all stores will be open an extra hour today!"

Crazy Mose, who sold hats, scratched his head. "But they're already open twenty-four hours a day."

The mayor looked at Crazy Mose as if he were *crazy.*

"Fine!" he declared. "I decree that from now on days will be twenty-five hours long!"

"And they call *me* crazy," muttered Crazy Mose.

With that, the mayor and Who Bris departed.

Cindy Lou tugged at her father's sleeve once more.

"Dad, who's the Grinch?" she asked.

Lou looked around nervously.

"Cindy Lou, we should talk about this later," he muttered. "I've got to get to work . . . and you've got to get to school."

"Is it true that he really doesn't like Chris—" Cindy Lou began.

"School! Go to school!" Lou shouted, giving Cindy Lou a little shove.

Cindy Lou sighed, shrugged, and walked off.

As she did . . .

- The wheels fell off a bicycle just behind her;
- Crazy Mose, who was carrying a large stack of hats, tripped over something and collapsed;
- two Who children ran by carrying a

dangerous-looking hacksaw;

- the baker's holiday cookies were ruined by a defective cookie cutter;
- an old Who sat in what he thought was a chair and ended up splayed out on the sidewalk;
- and a marble rolled into the middle of Main Street, sending ninety-three Whos flying (thirty-three of them ended up in the emergency room of Whoville General Hospital for annoying bumps and bruises).

Whoville had been Grinched. And it was only the beginning . . .

6

LATER THAT SAME DAY, Cindy Lou Who sat in Miss Rue Who's first-grade class, wondering why she wasn't feeling particularly Christmas cheer–full.

"All right, class," said Miss Rue Who, "I'd like to hear what subjects you've chosen for your Wholiday class projects."

Cindy Lou stared out the window as her best friend, Sophie, stood up to speak.

"The Wholiday class project I've chosen is

'The Origins of the Santy Claus,'" said Sophie solemnly.

Next in line to volunteer was Casper Boo Who.

"My topic is 'Searching for Presents—How I Locked Myself in the Attic for Three Days. A Survivor's Tale.'"

The class gasped politely.

Then Miss Rue Who turned to Cindy Lou.

Cindy Lou stood up and took a deep breath.

"I propose," she said clearly, "to resolve a question no one in Whoville seems willing to answer."

"Why do crayons look so good but taste so bad?" asked Casper.

"No," Cindy Lou replied. "Who is the Grinch, and why doesn't he like Christmas?"

Every single window shade in the entire Whoville Elementary School snapped up. The jaws of every single child in Cindy Lou's class dropped to the floor. Miss Rue Who dropped her ruler and turned a lovely shade of chartreuse. (Look it up.)

"Cindy Lou Who!" she snapped. "We do not discuss that sort of thing at school."

"What?" Cindy Lou said, puzzled. "All I said was Gr—"

"Aaaaah!" Miss Rue Who shrieked.

Cindy Lou sat down.

Three hours later, Lou Lou Who arrived at school, flustered and out of breath. He found Cindy Lou seated at her desk with her head down, and Miss Rue Who pacing the floor of her classroom, looking rather upset.

"Miss Rue Who? I heard you were keeping my daughter after school, and I—"

"Sit down, Lou," snapped Miss Rue Who.

Lou sat.

"Mr. Lou Who," Miss Rue Who continued, "your daughter . . . your daughter . . . she, well, she said . . . oh, my . . ."

"All I said," Cindy Lou piped up, "was that I want to do my Christmas report on the Grinch."

The window shades in Whoville Elementary School snapped up again.

Lou got to his feet and went up to Miss Rue Who's desk.

"Look, Miss Rue Who," he babbled. "I'm sure we can straighten this whole thing out. Remember what a goof-off I was in school, and now look at me. I'm the postmaster of Whoville!" Lou stood up proudly—or as proudly as possible, given that the small school desk he had been sitting in was still attached to his derriere. (You can look that up, too. In fact, you really should.)

Miss Rue Who was not impressed. "By the way, Lou," she said icily, "did you ever find my package? You know . . . the important one? That was guaranteed to be delivered? Regardless of rain, or snow, or sleet, or hail?"

Lou blushed. "No. No, I didn't."

Miss Rue Who stared down her nose at Lou. The silence stretched out to an extremely uncomfortable length.

"All right, then. Good-bye, Miss Rue Who," Lou finally said. "Uh, Cindy Lou, come help your old man out down at the post office."

Cindy Lou stood up and followed her father—the student desk still attached to his bottom—out of the classroom.

"And a merry Christmas to you!" Lou desperately threw over his shoulder as he and his daughter made their escape.

Three hours later, Cindy Lou and Lou were racing around the Whoville Post Office, taking Christmas packages from a host of Whos, all of whom were sending gifts out to friends and family—all of which were late.

"I need this there tomorrow!" shouted one.

"I need this there today!" insisted a second.

"I need this there yesterday!" babbled a third.

"All right, all right," Lou said soothingly,

grabbing package after package. "We'll send them all heckuvarush."

"Daddy, I'm sorry I got you in trouble," Cindy Lou said as her dad zoomed by.

"That's okay, honey," Lou said, zooming back the other way.

"But I don't understand," Cindy Lou went on. "Why won't anyone talk about the Grinch?"

"You see, Cindy Lou," Lou said, zooming past her once more, "the Grinch is a Who who . . . well, he's not really a Who, he's more of a . . . of a . . ."

"What?" asked Cindy Lou.

"Exactly!" said her father, relieved. "The Grinch is a What who doesn't like Christmas. I mean, look at his mailbox!"

Lou pointed at my mailbox. It had a wonderful spider web draped attractively across it, and it was neatly covered in dust.

"Not a single Christmas card in or out," Lou went on. *"Ever."*

"But why?" Cindy Lou wanted to know.

But before her father could answer, Mayor May Who stormed into the post office.

"Postmaster Lou Who?" he bellowed. "I just got my mail, and we've got a bit of a problem here. These letters are addressed to almost everyone in this town except me!"

He handed a large stack of letters to the bewildered Lou.

"*The Book of Who* is very clear about this subject, Lou," the mayor went on. "Who Bris?"

Who Bris, who was standing just behind the mayor—you'll notice that Who Bris *always* stands just behind the mayor—handed May Who *The Book of Who*, opened to the appropriate page.

"'Since Christmas cards are sent by mail, the postal service must never fail,'" May Who read. He looked up at Lou. "I certainly hope you find *every* letter."

"If you'd like to keep your job, you better," Who Bris rhymed. May Who pinched him.

"Yes, sir," Lou said nervously.

"Merry Christmas!" the mayor said cheerily as he stormed out again. Who Bris followed him at a discreet distance.

Lou stared at the stack of letters in his hands.

"That's strange," he muttered to himself. "I sorted everything myself . . ."

Actually, it wasn't strange at all. I had just Grinched the post office.

As a matter of fact, I was there on the scene at that very moment—putting the wrong mail into the wrong slots, sending nasty letters to all (chain letters, blackmail notes, jury duty notices), and generally enjoying myself.

"Would you mind helping me sort this mail, my little elf?" Lou asked Cindy Lou.

Cindy Lou started putting the mail into slots. She had just passed my own mail slot when she caught a glimpse of something in the back room. Oops. It was me.

She headed around the mail slots, where,

of course, she didn't find me. No one finds me unless I *want* to be found.

Well, almost no one.

Cindy Lou looked up.

There I was, clinging to the ceiling, holding Max by the collar.

She screamed.

I screamed.

Then I dropped to the floor.

"Hello," I said.

"You're the . . . you're the . . . ," Cindy Lou gasped.

"The Grinch." I nodded, smiling. And let me tell you—a Grinch smiling is a terrible sight to behold.

Cindy Lou stepped back and fell into the package funnel.

"Help!" she shrieked as her small body was propelled toward the stamping machine on the wide post office conveyor belt.

Of course, no one could hear her cries—it

was Christmas at the Whoville Post Office. Meaning, it was total chaos.

And, of course, *I* wasn't about to help her out.

"Let's go home, Max," I told my faithful canine companion. "I believe our work here is finished."

In answer, my faithful canine companion buried *his* canines in my rear.

"Hmmm," I said through gritted teeth. "Do I sense your disapproval?"

Max dug *his* teeth in deeper.

"Help!" cried Cindy Lou.

"O bleeding hearts of the world unite!" I groaned. Then I pulled Cindy Lou off the conveyor belt.

Max unburied his teeth. I rubbed my rear.

"Thanks for saving me!" Cindy Lou said gratefully.

"Saved you? I saved you? Oh, that's rich!" I began to chortle. "Aha-ha-ha! The Grinch saved a Who? Ha-ha-ha!"

After a while, Cindy Lou started to laugh, too.

Stupid child. Nobody laughs at the Grinch.

The next thing Cindy Lou knew, she was tied up neatly like a package ready to be delivered. Hopefully, to the North Pole.

"All wrapped up with no place to go. That is what Christmas is all about for you Whos, isn't it?" I sniffed. "Presents."

"Cindy Lou? It's time to go home," Lou called from the front room.

By the time he reached his darling daughter, I was gone.

"Cindy Lou?" Lou looked around.

Cindy Lou popped her arms out of the package she was wrapped in and quickly untied herself.

"What happened?" Lou asked.

"Uh . . . I accidentally wrapped myself up," Cindy Lou lied.

"That happens to me almost every day," Lou sighed. "Come on. Let's go home."

I watched them from a safe distance as they trudged down the street.

Saved her? Saved her, indeed! I'll show her . . . I'll show everyone in Whoville!

Just you wait . . .

7

WHEN CINDY LOU AND LOU Lou Who got home, the house was dark.

"No lights on in the house," Lou said redundantly as he opened the door. "Your mom must be out shopping."

"Up here, honey!" a voice called from somewhere above their heads.

Lou and Cindy Lou looked up toward the roof of the house. There, perched on a ladder, wearing her housecoat and galoshes, was Lou's wife and Cindy Lou's mother—that's just one person, mind you—Betty Lou Who. She was busy draping a gigantic string of Christmas lights onto the already overlit roof.

"I can feel it, Lou!" Betty proclaimed. "This is the year. When the judges read the name of the lighting contest winner, they're going to cry out, 'Mrs. Betty Lou Who!'" She beamed at the thought. "Hand me those lights, Lou!"

Lou picked up the lights that Betty was pointing to and handed them to his wife.

"Isn't this the chandelier from the dining room, dear?" he inquired.

"There are no lights in here!" Cindy Lou called from inside the house.

"It's all for the cause!" Betty chirped merrily as she stapled the dining room's chandelier to the roof of the house. "Feel your way around, dear. Oh, and could you be Mommy's little helper, Cindy Lou, and unscrew the bulb from the refrigerator?"

"And be careful with those presents, Cindy Lou!" her father added.

"Sure," muttered their daughter as she stumbled over the coat tree in the dark hallway. "Presents. I guess that's what Christmas is all about."

"Every year, Martha May Whovier wins the contest," Betty went on as she stapled some more lights onto the roof. "Well, not this year. This year, I'm going to beat that prim, perfect little—"

"Oh, Betty!"

Betty turned. Standing on the porch of her delightfully decorated little house just across the street stood prim, perfect little Martha May Whovier.

"Martha May!" Betty said sweetly, driving a staple into her thumb.

"My, I've never seen so many beautiful Christmas lights, Betty!" cooed Martha May.

"Oh, I'd blow every fuse if I tried to keep up with you, Martha May!" Betty responded cheerily. "You color-coordinated crag . . . ," she added under her breath.

Martha May picked up a small box and opened it. She waved it at Betty.

"Aren't these antique lights darling? They're handcrafted and almost a hundred years old," she called.

She hung the string of charming little lights over her doorway.

Then she pulled out a dangerous-looking giant light gun.

"This, on the other hand," she said crisply, "is new."

And she began firing lights onto her house. *Bam! Bam! Bam!*

When she was finished, she blew across the barrel of her light gun, put it back in its holster, and smiled cheerfully.

"Well, good night, Betty. Good luck in the contest. And by the way . . . you're strangling your husband."

Betty looked down to where Lou was

tangled up in a string of Christmas lights.

"Aaaaaargh," said Lou.

"Oops," said Betty.

Martha May took a swig of eggnog as she stepped around to the back of the house. "It's Christmas *somewhere,"* she muttered to herself.

Just then, Mayor May Who's voice boomed out from down the block.

"Why, hello, Martha May!" he called.

"Why, hello, Martha May." Can't the idiot think of anything original to say?

Martha May looked down her nose at him.

"August. To what do I owe the pleasure?" she asked.

Pleasure. Hah.

"Well, I was . . . you know . . . out and about . . . and, um, just thought I'd—"

"Ask you out!" Who Bris popped in.

"You know, this is sort of my deal," May Who whispered furiously, kicking Who Bris in the kneecap.

"I won't be a third wheel!" Who Bris

protested, rubbing his knee.

"Oh, look!" the mayor said brightly, glaring at Who Bris. "You're about to lose a button on your coat."

May Who ripped a button off Who Bris's coat and flung it down the street into a snow-bank.

Who Bris took off after his button.

"Hey, Lou!" he said cheerfully as he passed Lou's house. "Merry Christmas!" he added, blinking at Betty's wired domicile.

"Urgle argle!" Lou said cheerfully as Betty continued to unwrap Christmas lights from around his neck.

Now, *that's* what I call Christmas spirit.

Not!

I had been looking forward to making some crank phone calls this evening. But after this disgusting display of cheerfulness, crank phone calls were not going to be enough. This year, the Whos were going to get more . . . much more. I'd tie up the entire phone system before I was through!

I was going to figure out a way to ruin Christmas in Whoville if it was the last thing I did.

8

CINDY LOU WHO was in her dark room in her dark house. Well, she did have a flashlight. Or she would, as long as her mother didn't find it and staple it to the roof of the house.

A disturbingly cheerful little Christmas ditty was twirling around on her record player. She turned the speed down. Good. The song slowed, becoming melancholy and dreary.

Better, thought Cindy Lou. *Just how I feel.*

Lou and Betty Lou Who popped their heads into Cindy Lou's room.

"That's a beautiful song, Cindy Lou. But I think you're playing it on the wrong speed," said Lou. He adjusted Cindy Lou's record player, which began spewing out the cheerful Christmas ditty once again.

"Now hand over the flashlight, sweetie," said Betty. "Every bulb counts. Maybe you want to help Mommy lease an arc welder tomorrow?"

Cindy Lou shook her head. "No thanks. Mom, Dad, I'm going on a personal journey of enlightenment."

"But it's past your bedtime!" said Betty.

Cindy Lou shook her head. "Not *that* kind of journey, Mom. I'm doing my school report on . . . the Grinch."

Betty and Lou Lou Who gasped.

The phone rang.

Lou grabbed for it.

"Hello?" he said. "What did you say? Is my

subzero chillibrator running? I suppose so . . .”

I laughed. “Then you’d better go catch it!” I told him.

One of the oldest crank phone calls in the book . . . but it still gets ’em every time!

I hung up the phone and looked around at my dwelling.

Home, *stinky* home.

Living near the town dump sure has its advantages.

I have this terrific collection of hazardous waste materials, for example. As I always say, one man’s compost heap is another man’s potpourri. (Here’s another one you should look up.)

I really think we made a difference down there in Whoville today, don’t you? They’re really squirming tonight. I have no doubt about it. Especially that little girl in the post office . . . I scared the skeezles out of her.

Strange that she didn’t rat on us, though.

Probably afraid of the reprisals.

Yes, I feel bad. Real bad. I'm all dead inside. And that reminds me . . . I better check the size of my heart in my special Grinch-o-meter.

Excellent! Down a size and a half!

No one calls me. No one visits me. No one has ever seen this dump except me and Max . . . and that's *exactly* how I like it.

There's no one to talk to . . . and that's fine with me, too!

Hello? Did you hear anything, Max?

Hello? Anybody there? Hello? Hello?

Oh, never mind! I don't need anyone to talk to!

Do I?

9

Cindy Lou Who knocked on the door of Clarinella and Rose Who Biddie's house.

Clarinella opened the door. She was a creaky old Who who had seen better days. Now she and Rose spent their time talking about those better days. This made for some very boring after-dinner conversations.

"Hello there, little girl," said Clarinella, squinting down at Cindy Lou. "Are you here to read to us?"

"No," said Cindy Lou. "I hear you know some things about the Grinch."

Clarinella's eyes brightened. Someone who actually wanted to know something about those better days! She grabbed Cindy Lou by the sleeve.

"Come in, child. Come in!" she said, smiling broadly. "This is going to be fun!"

Cindy Lou set up her microphone on a table in front of Clarinella and Rose.

"I want you to tell me everything you know about the Grinch," she began.

"Whoticus Finch? I haven't seen him in years," said Rose vaguely. "What a delightful man!"

"No, the *Grinch,*" Cindy Lou said, talking a little more loudly. "Where did he come from?"

Clarinella gave Cindy Lou a mischievous look. "He came the way all Who babies come. On calm nights, they drift down from the sky on little pumbrasellas."

Cindy Lou nodded and made a note.

"It was forty years ago this Christmas Eve," Clarinella went on.

"Whoticus's lady friend was out of town for the weekend, and he was feeling lonely," said Rose.

"Rose!" Clarinella gave Rose a dirty look. Then she turned back to Cindy Lou. "As I was saying, it was Christmas Eve, and a strange wind blew that night . . .

"We were having our annual holiday get-together. It was a little . . . noisy, I'm afraid." Clarinella sniffed apologetically. "It wasn't until the next morning that anybody realized the little Grinch was outside the house, poor dear . . ." Clarinella shook her head solemnly. "We knew right away he was . . . special."

"Yes," Rose sighed. "Whoticus was a strong man, but gentle. He had a tattoo of—"

"Rose!" Clarinella kicked Rose under the table. "We're talking about the Grinch!"

"Who?" Rose murmured vaguely.

Clarinella shook her head. Then she turned

back to Cindy Lou. "Anyway . . . he was a wonderful little . . . whatever he was . . . and we raised him like any other Who child. He went to the same school you do, Cindy Lou—and if I'm not mistaken, he had Miss Rue Who as a teacher, too. Little Martha May Whovier was in his class, as I recall . . . wasn't she, Rose?"

"Oh, he was," Rose gushed. "A classy figure of a man, Whoticus was . . ."

Cindy Lou's next stop was Martha May Whovier's house.

"The Grinch?" Martha May said casually. "I may have gone to school with him, although I can hardly remember. I didn't have time to socialize. I was far too busy with my studies . . ."

Wait! I must interrupt myself! How cruel! How can she not remember? The way she looked at me . . . the way she licked her lollipop and batted her eyes! Even May Who was jealous!!!

I remember what she said to me . . . "You know, Christmas is my favorite day of the year. I just love the colors—the red . . . and the green."

She touched my arm when she said "the green"! And you know what color my fur is!!!

She liked me. I know it!

And that's why I made the angel ornament for the school's Christmas gift exchange . . . especially for her.

It took me all night and the entire contents of the Who Biddies' silverware drawer.

And that's not all. I even . . . I even . . . shaved for her.

It was May Who's fault!!! Always taunting me . . . always teasing me . . . telling the teacher I was shedding! Telling me I would never look nice because I was only eight years old and I already had a beard!!!

So I borrowed Clarinella's electric razor.

And I made a complete and total mess of myself.

And all the students laughed at me. Including Martha May!

Stupid Christmas! Stupid presents! I showed them! I trashed their stupid little Christmas tree! I ruined their Christmas celebration! And I never looked back! I moved up to Mt. Crumpit and I never looked back!

You tell 'em, Max! I never looked back! Right? Not ever!

"Yes, Cindy Lou." Mayor May Who shook his head solemnly. "The Grinch made it very clear that day he wanted no part of our Christmas celebration, and that he despised our Who warmth and generosity. Ow!" May Who hauled off and whacked Who Bris, who was giving him a manicure and had accidentally stabbed him in the elbow.

"And, in fact, that was the last time we ever saw him," the mayor continued.

Cindy Lou nodded sadly.

"You know, Cindy Lou, there are other,

more suitable, role models for a young girl such as yourself. Perhaps someone who holds an elected office. Interesting fact about me, they had to take my tonsils out twice. You see, they . . . Cindy Lou? Cindy Lou?"

But Cindy Lou had disappeared.

Mayor May Who nodded. "I think I talked some sense into her." He looked around for Who Bris. "How about a massage?"

IT WAS TIME for the Whobilation.

I was staring down at the town through my Grinchy periscope.

Nutcrackers!! A cute little Who boy just gave the entire contents of his piggy bank to the Whovation Army!!! And . . . oh, no! I can't look! He's giving them his pacifier, too!

Such kindness must not go unpunished. And I'm just the Grinch to take him across my knee and give him a good spanking!

Hmmm. There go Lou and his family. They must be on the way to the Holiday Cheermeister nominations. I can't imagine anything I'd like less than to be Holiday Cheermeister. Holiday Gloommeister would be more like it.

I simply have to figure out a way to stop all of this Whovian good cheer! But how?

Lou peered at the small slip of paper he held in his hand as he, Cindy Lou, Stu, and Drew tramped over to the town square for the nominations.

"I . . . Lou Lou Who," he read, "humble postmaster of Whoville, hold for applause, do hereby—smile, eye contact, make them think that this is your own idea—hereby spontaneously . . . hmmm. Spon-ta-NEE-us-ly? SPON-ta-nee-us-ly? Spon-TA-nee-us-ly?" Lou stopped. "Cindy Lou, what does *spon-ta-NEE-us-ly* mean?"

"All of a sudden," said Cindy Lou. "Without planning it."

The countdown to Christmas in Whoville.

Keeping an eye on would-be visitors.

Cindy Lou Who

Miss Rue Who

Betty Lou Who gets ready for the lighting contest.

The Grinch is
just not like other
Who children.

The Grinch and Martha May Whovier—
childhood sweethearts.

The Whobilation

Clarinella and
Rose Whobiddie
at the Whobilation.

The Wholiday
Cheermeister

Preparing to steal Christmas.

The Grinch steals Christmas.

The Lou Whos discover the true meaning of Christmas.

A Christmas moment.

Christmas returned!

Merry Christmas,
Mr. Grinch . . .

. . . and a merry Christmas to all!

"Oh," said her father. He looked down at his notes again. "I spon-TA-nee-us-ly . . . uh . . . nominate my employer, Mayor August May Who, for Holiday Cheermeister."

"Dad?" Cindy Lou tugged on her father's sleeve. "I've been thinking about the Whobilation . . . and I wanted to warn you. I may do something drastic."

"Great, dear," Lou said absently, trying to memorize his nomination speech. "Go ask your mother."

Cindy Lou looked around.

"Where'd Mom go?" she asked.

Just then, she heard a terrible crash. It sounded as if someone had removed the traffic light on Main and Green streets, causing a five-car collision.

"Here I am!" Betty appeared, dragging a traffic light behind her. "I just found the cutest light for my Christmas display!"

Cindy Lou rolled her eyes.

"Hurry up!" Betty went on. "We'll be late!"

The whine of a police siren blended with the sounds of some Christmas carolers bellowing "Deck the Halls" as Cindy Lou and her family entered the town square.

Mayor May Who stood at the podium, wearing his red-and-green plaid sash, his famous antler hat (complete with moss and holly), and his red puttees. (You really must look that one up if you want to get the full picture.)

May Who held up his hand for quiet, and the large crowd of Whos who had already gathered slowly settled down.

"And now," May Who proclaimed, "the nominations for that Who among us who best typifies the qualities of who-dom and who-dery. The Whoville Holiday Cheermeister!!!"

Hearty cheers broke out among the assembled Whos.

"Do I hear a nomina—" May Who began. But before he could finish, Lou Lou Who was on his feet.

"I," Lou read slowly, "Lou Lou Who, humble postmaster of Whoville, hold for applause, do hereby—smile, eye contact, make them think this is your own idea—"

"I nominate the Grinch!" a small voice piped up.

All the Whos in the town square gasped in horror.

Mayor May Who looked around and down, trying to locate the offending voice.

It was the voice of Cindy Lou.

Mayor May Who frowned.

"My, my," he said in a particularly oily voice. "What an altruistic daughter you have there, Lou."

"Uh . . . uh . . . thank you," said Lou. He turned to Betty worriedly. "Altru-*what?*" he whispered. "That's good, right?"

"Well," said May Who expansively, already knowing the answer to his next question, "do I hear a second for . . . for . . . the Grinch?"

There was dead silence in the square.

Cindy Lou looked around. Wasn't there anyone to support her? Wouldn't anybody second her nomination?

Obviously not.

"Right," said May Who briskly. "Cindy Lou, let me quote a verse from our *Book of Who—*"

Who Bris popped up behind the mayor and handed him his copy of *The Book of Who,* opened to the appropriate page.

"'The term "Grinchy" will apply,'" May Who continued, "'when Christmas spirit is in short supply.'"

May Who snapped the book shut, gave it back to Who Bris, and looked up at Cindy Lou.

"I ask you, Cindy Lou," he went on. "Does that sound like our Holiday Cheermeister?"

"True, Mayor May Who," Cindy Lou said. "But *The Book of Who* says this, too." Cindy Lou quoted from memory, "'No matter how different a Who may appear, he'll always be welcomed with Holiday Cheer.'"

Who Bris desperately rustled through the pages of his copy of *The Book of Who,* looking for Cindy Lou's quotation. Sure enough, there it was, on page 35.

May Who grabbed the book out of Who Bris's hands.

"But the Book also says, 'The award cannot go to the Grinch because . . . because . . .'"

He flipped through the book, desperately trying to find a quote that would serve his purpose.

"'Because . . . sometimes . . . things get . . . lead-pipe cinch!'" he finally said triumphantly.

"You made that up!" Cindy Lou shouted indignantly. "It doesn't say that!"

"Yes, it does!" said May Who.

"What page?" Cindy Lou asked.

May Who shut the book on Who Bris's finger. "Oops. Lost my place. But it's in there."

Cindy Lou shook her head and kept fighting. "The Book *does* say, 'The Cheermeister is one who deserves a backslap or a toast. It goes to the soul at Christmas who needs it most!'"

She turned to the crowd of astonished Whos.

"And I believe that soul is the Grinch! And if you're the Whos I hope you are, you will, too."

For a moment, the crowd was still. Then a small sniffle could be heard somewhere in the back. Then one or two Whos began to clap. And then the entire congregation of Whos started to applaud brave little Cindy Lou.

"Fine, fine," said Mayor May Who, flustered. "If you people want to waste a perfectly good nomination, go ahead. But the Grinch will never come down."

"And when he doesn't," Who Bris chimed in, "the mayor will wear the crown."

"More or less," May Who said hurriedly.

"Now, let's just concentrate on having the best Christmas ever!"

The Whos all cheered again.

Cindy Lou looked up at Mt. Crumpit.

It was all very well to nominate the Grinch for Holiday Cheermeister, she was thinking. But how was she going to get me to come down to Whoville and accept the job?

11

I WAS HAVING a restless night. All the cheering and caroling and merriment drifting up to Mt. Crumpit from Whoville was giving me bad dreams.

The worst drcam of all was that a cute little girl was climbing up Mt. Crumpit to see me.

Have I mentioned that I particularly detest cute little girls?

And what's worse, she was escaping all my booby traps, especially designed to keep Whos out of my inner sanctum. She had already gotten past the Terrifying Spring-Release Trees, the Boulder Avalanche, the Chalk-Scratching-on-a-Blackboard torture device . . .

And then she was knocking on my door!

(A moment here. You might ask how I know all this, since I've just told you I was asleep. Well, chalk it up to poetic license. Anyway, I'm *writing this book—you're just reading it. So keep your ridiculous questions to yourself.)*

Cindy Lou—for the cute little girl was, of course, Cindy Lou—knocked at my door.

Of course, I didn't answer it.

So she walked in.

Just like a Who—barging in where she's not wanted.

"Mr. Grinch?" she called.

I had my head buried under seventeen pillows so that I wouldn't have to listen to the Whoville caroler's weapon of choice—the tenth verse of "The Twelve Days of

Christmas." So, of course, I didn't hear her.

"Mr. Grinch?" she called again. Then she saw me.

She tapped me on the shoulder.

"Hello, little girl," I said. "HOW DARE YOU ENTER THE GRINCH'S LAIR??? YOU LITTLE MICRO-MENACE!!! THE IMPUDENCE! THE AUDACITY!!! THE UNMITIGATED GALL!!! YOU WILL RUE THE DAY YOU CAME HERE!!!!

"YOU CALLED DOWN THE THUNDER. NOW GET READY FOR THE BOOM! GAZE INTO THE FACE OF . . . FEAR!!!!!!"

Well, *I* was impressed.

"Mr. Grinch, my name is Cindy Lou," she said, standing her ground.

"You see?" I stared deeply into her eyes. "Terror is welling up inside of you."

"I'm not scared," said Cindy Lou.

I was stumped . . . but only for a second.

"Denial is to be expected in the face of true fear," I responded, with a gloating smile.

Let's see her counter that one!

"I don't think so," she said.

But I was on a roll now. I didn't hesitate.

"Doubt!" I gloated. "The second sign of true terror. Now you're doomed. Raaaaaah! I'm gonna . . . whoooooo! And then . . . hooooooo! I'm a psycho! Homicide, homicide," I chanted. "Hold me back, Max! Hold me back!"

Cindy Lou just stood therc.

Kids today are so desensitized.

"What do you want?" I finally asked her.

"Mr. Grinch, I came to invite you to be Holiday Cheermeister" was the little fiend's reply.

"Holiday who-bie what-ie?" was all I could muster. I admit it—I was floored.

"Cheermeister," she repeated.

Ha-ha. That was rich. The little devil actually wanted me to go down to Whoville to be the Holiday Cheermeister!

"Maybe I'm not hearing you correctly," I taunted her.

"I know you hate Christmas," Cindy Lou began, "but what if it's all just a misunderstanding?"

"Don't care," I told her.

"I mean," she barreled on, "I myself am having some yuletide doubts . . . but maybe if you can reunite with the Whos and be a part of Christmas . . . then maybe it will be all right for me, too."

"I'm sorry," I sneered. "Your hour is up. Please make another appointment with the receptionist on your way out."

That got to her.

"Please, please," she begged. "You have to accept the award."

It was an *award?*

"It's an award?" I asked her. "You didn't mention it was an award."

"With a trophy and everything." Cindy Lou could sense an opening, and she took advantage of it.

"And I won?"

"You won," she confirmed.

"So that means there were losers." This was getting interesting. "A town full of losers. I like that. Was anyone emotionally shattered? Come on. A minute ago I couldn't shut you up. Details, details!"

"The mayor wasn't very happy," Cindy Lou admitted.

"Awwww." I made a sympathetic face.

"Martha May Whovier will be there," Cindy Lou went on, with an innocent look.

"Oh, she will, will she?" I was beginning to see the possibilities. "And she'll see me—the winner. She'll be all over me like fleegle flies on a flat-faced floogle horse. Well, I'm sorry to disappoint you, Martha May baby, but the G-train has left the station. Next stop, fame, fortune, palimony, and glorious isolation!"

"So, will you come?" asked Cindy Lou.

It took me a second.

"Why not? I don't know whether it's the adorable twinkle in your eye, or that nonconformist streak that reminds me of a younger, less hairy me, but you've convinced me. Who knows? This Whobilation could change my entire outlook on life."

"Really?" asked Cindy Lou, pleased.

"NO!!!!" I screamed, pulling a lever that opened a trapdoor right under her feet. She disappeared with a yelp.

"Did you see that!" I crowed to Max. "I outwitted a little girl! Yeah!"

Max was not impressed. And to tell you the truth, neither was I.

"What's their game?" I wondered out loud, examining the invitation that Cindy Lou had left behind. "Listen to this, Max. 'You are cordially invited.' *Cordially?* What do they mean by that? No one 'cordially' invites the Grinch! It should be 'with great trepidation and deepest regrets.' I'm sure they don't even really want me there."

Max barked.

"Besides," I ranted on, "how dare they

invite me down there on such short notice? Even if I wanted to go, my schedule wouldn't allow it.

"But . . . what would I wear?"

Max snorted and retired to the corner.

I started to look through my wardrobe. Maybe I could find something . . .

A straitjacket?

A kilt?

("It is *not* a dress, Max. It's a *kilt!!!*")

An iron stove?

A beehive?

The lederhosen and feathered hat of that annoying yodeler who happens to be singing his off-key ditties just outside my cave door?

That will do just fine.

And if he freezes to death? Well, that's his problem. He's the one who chose to go outside on a freezing night and yodel.

I must admit . . . I don't look half bad.

I look ALL bad.

Tee-hee.

All right. I'll pop in for a minute, allow them to envy me, grab a few popcorn shrimp, and blow out of there.

But what if it's a cruel prank? What if it's a cash bar? How dare they! That's it. I'm not going!

All right. I'll go, but I'll be fashionably late.

No.

Yes.

No.

Yes.

Yes.

Definitely no.

Well, okay, I'll go.

Ha! I had my fingers *crosssssssed!!!!!!*

I might have had my fingers crossed . . . or maybe I didn't. In either case, Max had had enough. He pulled the lever, and I plunged through the trapdoor . . . toward Whoville and my destiny.

12

WHILE I WAS GETTING all dolled up and ready to drop in on the Whobilation, Cindy Lou (remember her, the one who invited me in the first place?) was popping out of the Dumpster in the middle of town. Lucky for her, she landed safely in a snowbank.

"Oh, there you are!" said her father, who was just passing by. "Come on. The lighting contest's about to start!"

Lou grabbed his daughter's hand and

pulled her down the street. Cindy Lou looked back over her shoulder at Mt. Crumpit.

I wonder if he'll come, she thought wistfully.

When they reached their own street, they found the whole town gathered to witness the awarding of the prize for the best Christmas light display in Whoville.

"On this one thousandth Whobilation," Mayor May Who was saying, "where would we be without the magic and gaiety of Christmas lights?"

"Nowhere," Who Bris obediently replied.

"Yes," May Who said, stepping hard on Who Bris's foot. "Now, let's hear it for our Home Lighting Contest finalists!"

He pointed to Cindy Lou's house, which was uncharacteristically dark.

"Betty Lou Who," May Who proclaimed. "Mother of the little girl who invited the Grinch. Hit it, Betty!"

Betty took a deep breath and pulled her

switch, and the entire house lit up in a magnificent display that was unparalleled in the history of Christmas.

She had bought out all the local hardware stores, and in addition to every light in her own house and the aforementioned traffic signal, she had the local Quik-Mart sign, the local dry cleaner's sign, every stop sign in the town, and the light from the top of the town's one police car tacked up on her roof.

There was a small smattering of applause.

"And now," Mayor May Who proclaimed, "let's put your Who hands together for . . . your very own . . . Martha May Whovier!"

The Who band struck up a tune. Martha May Whovier pulled her switch.

And her house lit up in an even more spectacular—and, of course, tasteful—display than Betty's.

The crowd went wild.

Betty stared, dejected, at the house across the street.

But she wasn't ready to give up . . . not yet.

"Well, Martha May," she bellowed, "it looks like you beat me again . . . except this old gal's got a lot more lights left in her, lady!"

Betty started a gas generator. She plugged in five large plugs and flipped an even bigger switch than before . . .

And her house went crazy.

It was the most amazing display of lights that anyone had ever seen anywhere.

The crowd went even more wild than they had for Martha May's.

Mayor May Who looked torn. There was Betty's extraordinary house . . . and there was Martha May Whovier, looking a little dejected. She flashed him a tremulous smile.

The Who Lighting Committee judges handed May Who an envelope.

"And the winner is . . . ," he began, opening it up.

The name he read in the envelope was

Betty Lou Who's. The name he announced as the winner was—"Martha May Whovier!"

Betty's mouth dropped open.

Martha May stepped up and took a trophy from the outstretched hands of Mayor May Who. "Thank you so much," she gushed. "I'll display this trophy very proudly in my living room. Of course, the gold will throw off the whole color scheme, but I am willing to redecorate. Thank you."

Betty shook her head. How could this have happened? She had put everything she had into this year's lighting display . . . literally. As well as a few things that weren't technically hers.

Who Bris took the confused judges on the Who Lighting Committee off to one side and pressed large sums of money into each of their palms.

"Let's keep the name of the real winner of the contest between ourselves," he muttered as he sent them packing.

A dark cloud hung over Betty Lou Who's head. It threatened to rain all over Martha May Whovier's house.

"I was soft," Betty muttered. "I didn't want it enough. Next year, I train harder, start earlier—tomorrow, maybe—"

Cindy Lou shook her head for the umpteenth time. Something was very wrong here. She could feel it.

She wondered if anything could help.

In particular, she wondered if *I*, the Grinch, could help.

13

THE WHOS WERE GATHERED at the town square for the presentation of the Holiday Cheermeister of the Year award.

Mayor May Who stood at the podium.

"Well, it's time to present the Holiday Cheermeister of the Year award. Congratulations, Mr. Grinch."

He gestured to the empty chair beside him.

"He's not here?" May Who said in mock surprise. "He didn't show? Who could have predicted this? Well, we can't wait forever if we're to have—what, people?"

"THE BEST CHRISTMAS EVER!" shouted the crowd of Whos.

"Well," May Who went on, "I guess the award goes to the runner-up."

May Who snapped his fingers. Who Bris stepped up to the microphone.

"That's right," simpered Who Bris. "A man for whom Christmas comes not once a year, but every minute of every day. A handsome, noble man. A man who has had his tonsils removed twice—"

May Who grabbed the mike. "Interesting story. You see, they—"

But Mayor May Who was not destined to finish his story. (Not in *my* book, he's not!)

At that very moment, I blasted out of the Dumpster, went flying across to the town square, careened into the bass drum of the Whoville Marching Band, bounced off, flew into the 1,000th Whobilation banner, and was flung onto the stage and into the arms of . . . of . . . Martha May Whovier.

I knocked her flat.

I've always had that effect on Martha May.

"He made it!" Cindy Lou shouted happily.

"Martha May!" I said, pulling my nose out of her chest. "You look positively . . . buoyant this evening!"

The crowd was completely silent.

"Boo," I said.

Everybody screamed and moved back a step.

It's nice to know I still have that kind of an effect on people.

"Ooh, hot crowd, hot crowd," I said, grabbing the mike. "Now, about that award . . . and the little girl mentioned a check."

"No, I didn't," said Cindy Lou.

Mayor May Who recovered himself first.

"Don't you worry, Holiday Cheermeister, you'll get your award. But first a little family reunion. They nursed you, they clothed you—

here they are . . . your old Biddies!"

Clarinella and Rose Who Biddie rushed up onto the stage.

I was surprised they were still alive.

"My, haven't you turned out to be a handsome, odd-looking whatever-you-are!" Clarinella gushed.

"We've missed you," said Rose, hugging Who Bris.

"Rose!" admonished Clarinella.

Then, before I could defend myself, she whipped out a sweater and rammed it over my head.

It was pretty hideous . . . and five sizes too small.

"It's for you, dear," said Clarinella. "What do you think of it?"

"Do you know what I think of it?" I sputtered. "It's—"

Cindy Lou gave me a look.

"It's . . . it's . . . just what I always wanted," I forced myself to say.

Cindy Lou gave me a thumbs-up sign. Why was I paying attention to her, anyway?

May Who stepped forward again.

"And now, Cheermeister, to your duties!" he said.

"Huh?" I asked.

"Bring on the Chair of Cheer!" he proclaimed.

"Put him in the Chair of Cheer! The Chair of Cheer! The Chair of Cheer!" the Whos chanted.

I was shoved into a wooden chair. It was a pretty hard and uncheerful chair, if you ask me. But clearly no one was asking me.

"Not the Chair of Cheer!" I began. "The Chair may be too much, too soon—"

But the crowd had already picked the Chair up and carried me off.

Hmm. Hero worship. Maybe this wouldn't be too bad, after all.

"Out of the way. Cheermeister coming through!

"Put your backs into it, you grunts!

"Happy now, Cindy Lou?"

Mayor May Who interrupted my musings.

"First," May Who proclaimed, "you'll put your taste buds to the test as you judge . . . the Who Pudding Cook Off!"

Three gigantic and revolting spoonfuls of some disgustingly sweet and gloppy substance were shoveled into my mouth.

"Christmas Conga!" May Who shouted next.

I was forced to lead a conga line through the town.

"The Who Pie Cook Off!"

More disgusting substances were shoveled into my mouth.

"Vigorous exercise!"

I actually participated in a sack race . . . and won!

"The Who Cake Cook Off!"

Even more disgusting substances were shoveled into my mouth.

"Time to bless the children!"

A thousand tiny Who children punched me in the stomach and jumped on my head.

"More Christmas Conga!"

Sing it with me! "I-am-gonna throw up, I-am-gonna throw up!"

"The Who Nog Off!"

Well, at least I set a new Who eggnog-drinking record . . . just before I threw up.

"A new Who record!" the Whos proclaimed.

"You mean there are records in Whoville for which Holiday Cheermeister throws up the most, too?" I asked.

"That's right," said Crazy Mose. "Throwing up represents the spirit of giving!"

And they call *me* crazy.

"Now," Mayor May Who said finally, "it's time for the moment we've all been waiting for . . ."

"Ah, yes," I wheezed. "My award and the check."

"There is no check," said May Who.

"Are you *sure?*" I scratched my head. "Because I really thought I heard someone mention—"

"No," said May Who. "It's time for the Christmas Present Pass It On!" May Who turned to Martha May. "Martha May?" he said, smiling sweetly.

Martha May turned and handed a beautifully wrapped present to Officer Wholihan, head of the Who police force. Wholihan turned and handed a present to Whoboy. And so on, and so on . . .

And I hadn't brought a present.

I searched desperately through my pockets for something, anything . . .

But, of course, they were empty.

Luckily, by the time the Present Pass It On passed on back to me, I had found the perfect gift.

"Here you are, Martha May," I said, handing her a man's large gold wristwatch. "I'm sorry I didn't have time to wrap it."

"That's my watch," May Who pointed out.

"Oh," I said. "So all of a sudden *everything* on your wrist belongs to you? Then you might as well take your cuff links back, too."

Mayor May Who gleefully faced the crowd.

"He's got nothing!" he shouted.

That's right—rub it in.

"But don't worry—we've got a little something for you, Grinch."

Who Bris held out a gift-wrapped box.

"The gift of . . . a Christmas shave!" Who Bris announced malevolently.

And he opened the box.

Nestled inside was an electric razor . . . just like the one I had used when I was eight! The one with which I had defaced myself!

I shivered.

"So . . . what do you have for Martha May?" May Who went on. "Oh, right, nothing. Well, luckily, I brought along a little something."

He whipped out a small wrapped box and handed it to Martha May.

She opened it.

Inside was a gigantic diamond ring.

"Please become Mrs. August May Who," the mayor begged, going down on one knee.

"Aw," said all the Whos.

"Oh, no," said Cindy Lou in a small voice.

She knew. She knew I was about to blow.

"Uh, August . . . I'm overwhelmed," said Martha May.

"But that's not all!" May Who continued. "If you agree to become Mrs. May Who, along with a lifetime supply of happiness, you'll also receive this brand-new . . . washer-dryer! You'll wash your new husband's clothes in style. From Whomana, maker of fine Who appliances. But wait . . . there's more! It's a brand-new . . . car! Generously provided by the taxpayers of Whoville! So what do you say, Martha May? You have ten seconds on the clock . . ."

Martha May just stood there, blinking.

“Well . . . I . . . these gifts are quite dazzling . . .”

That’s when I totally lost it.

“Of course they are!” I shrieked. “That’s what it’s always been about, isn’t it? Gifts! Gifts! Gifts! Well, let me tell you what happens to your gifts. They all end up coming to me . . . in your garbage! I could hang myself with all the bad Christmas neckties I’ve found at the dump!

“And, Mr. Pastry Chef, here’s a tip: no one likes the fruitcakes! They’re not even biodegradable! And in time, they can even become highly explosive!

“But what the hey. It’s better to give than to receive, right?”

I pointed to a Who in the audience.

“*That* Who got his wife a fryolator, while his secretary got a mink muzzle-nuzzle!

“*That* Who’s wife slapped him in the face.

“And his secretary is his wife’s sister . . . AND his wife is expecting!”

The crowd groaned.

"And *that* Who"—I pointed to another in the crowd—"switches price tags. And that one"—I pointed to another—"licks candy canes and puts them back!"

The crowd moaned.

"The avarice never ends. 'I want golf clubs. I want diamonds. I want a pony so I can ride it twice, get bored, and then sell it to make glue!' This whole Christmas season is stupid, stupid, stupid!"

The crowd gasped.

I turned to go.

"Mr. Grinch, wait! Don't go yet!" cried Cindy Lou.

I turned back again.

"Oh, that's right. I'm a terrible Cheermeister! I forgot the most important Cheermeister duty of them all—the lighting of the tree!"

That's when I set the Whoville Christmas tree on fire.

I think it was a masterful touch, don't you?

"Do something!" screamed Mayor May

Who to Who Bris as the Who fire trucks arrived on the scene. "To the Grinch!"

I took off. And the Whos took off after me.

Of course, they couldn't catch me.

I got to the Dumpster in record time.

And then I was home.

But I can't just leave it there. I've got to do something. Those Whos have to pay. I won't go through this pa-rum-pum-pum-pummeling again. Uh-uh. No, I won't.

I'm going to stop Christmas if it's the last thing I do.

14

"I JUST WANTED EVERYONE to be together for Christmas," Cindy Lou said in a tiny voice.

Mayor May Who looked contemptuously down at her.

"Good thing we have a spare Christmas tree," he said.

The new tree looked exactly like the old one. Who Bris lowered it in place.

The Whos all cheered.

Cindy Lou blinked back a tear as she walked from the town square.

She was not having a very merry Christmas at all.

15

IT DIDN'T TAKE ME LONG to come up with a plan. (Well, actually, it had taken about thirty-two years of thinking nonstop, but who's counting?)

I knew exactly what I was going to do.

It was despicable. It was disgusting.

It was de-lovely.

I had to use a lot of stuff that I had just lying around in my junk drawer to make the sleigh. (And since my junk drawer is actually my entire house, there was quite a lot of junk in it!)

I even made myself a designer license plate—MEAN 1. Cute, huh?

Of course, I didn't have any reindeer. Max would have to do.

"Here's your motivation," I told him. "You're Rudolph, you're different, you can't play any reindeer games. Then Santa picks you and you save Christmas—wait. No, you don't. Forget that part. We'll improvise. You *hate* Christmas. You're going to steal it. Saving Christmas was a lousy ending, totally unrealistic."

Max wasn't convinced. But, hey, I pay the vet bills.

By the time I sewed myself into the costume, tied the antlers on Max, and hitched him up to my ho-ho-ho-mobile, you couldn't tell me from the real thing.

If you were about five miles away, that is.

But it didn't matter—because nobody would be awake to see me, anyway.

"Fat Boy," I guessed, was just about finishing up for the night. Talk about a recluse. The guy in red only comes out once a year—but you don't see him catching any flak for it.

Well, he was going to get a black eye this year in Whoville—that was for sure. And he'd have me to blame for it.

"On, Basher and Crasher and Vomit and Blitzkrieg!" I sang merrily as I drove the sleigh off the top of Mt. Crumpit.

There were a few seconds of mortal terror as the sleigh plummeted to earth like a ten-ton boulder—but then the darn thing flew!

It was a miracle of aerodynamic engineering.

Soon we were over Whoville—about to make our first landing.

"Flaps, check. Airspeed, check. Breath, check."

The breath was negatory, but all other systems were go.

We made a perfect three-point landing on

the first Whoville roof, slid right across it, and ended up nose-down in a snowbank on the other side of the house.

"I meant to do that. It's all part of a plan. Don't worry, I came prepared," I assured Max.

He shook some snow out of his antlers and gave me a dirty look.

But he was suitably impressed when I took out my grappling hook and flung it up onto the roof.

I hauled us back up quick as a flash . . . and then I was ready to go down my first chimney.

It was a magical experience.

Of course, it took a few minutes to squeeze my way down . . . but I figured if "Fat Boy" could make it, I could, too.

And then I was in!

The first things to go were the little Who stockings, all hung in a row by the fireplace.

My wool-eating moths took care of *them.*

Then I turned on the special hose attachment on my vacuum cleaner and sucked up all the presents into my sleigh.

It was a nice haul.

Oh, I had fun that night. Sometimes, I went down the chimney. Sometimes, I went up through the floor, sawing a hole underneath the Christmas tree and letting it fall gently into my clutches. The whole thing went off without a hitch. My sack of Who presents got bigger and bigger. Max wheezed more and more as he dragged my sleigh from Who house to Who house.

I even stole the Christmas presents in the Who children's dreams.

No security system could stop me. No guard dog could prevent me. The operation was charmed from the start.

I even managed to set up a booby trap for Mayor May Who.

Would *he* be surprised when he woke up.

Martha May Whovier looked lovely in her sleep.

And then I got to Cindy Lou Who's house.

First I totally destroyed the swing set her father had built her as a present. (It wasn't hard to do—I had already fouled things up by replacing the instructions with some of my own. The thing was as flimsy as a house of cards.)

Then I made a clean sweep of all the presents.

Then I went to the refrigerator and cleaned out the whole thing. And while I was at it, I took every box and jar in the cupboards, too.

I was developing quite an appetite.

I was just stuffing the Christmas tree up the chimney when I heard a voice.

"Excuse me?" it said.

I looked around the tree. It was Cindy Lou, rubbing the sleep from her eyes.

"Santa Claus," she said, "what are you doing with our tree?"

I had to do some fancy footwork, let me tell you.

I told her that I was taking the tree home with me to fix a defective light.

Would you believe that she bought it? Children are so gullible.

"I can't believe I'm actually looking at Santa Claus" was all the little tyke could manage.

"Well, here I am," I told her. "Santa Claus. I'm certainly not the Grinch, if that's what you were thinking." (I kicked myself under the mistletoe. Almost gave it away!) "Well . . . off to the South Pole!"

"Don't you mean the North Pole?" asked little Cindy Lou.

"Ho, ho, ho," I replied. "Right. See, the North Pole's being renovated. So I'm working out of the South Pole this year. Got a little time-share with the Tooth Fairy and, you know, Sasquatch. Good guy. I gotta go."

But Cindy Lou wanted to continue the conversation.

"Santa," she wanted to know, "what's Christmas really about?"

"Vengeance!" I said. "And, oh, presents, of course, obviously."

"I was afraid of that," Cindy Lou sighed.

I really needed to get out of there. So I got Cindy Lou a glass of water and hustled her off to bed.

"Santa?" she asked as she headed upstairs. "Don't forget the Grinch. I know he's mean and hairy and smelly. His hands may be cold and clammy. But I think he's actually kinda . . . sweet."

I gulped. "Sweet? You think he's . . . *sweet?*"

Cindy Lou nodded. "Merry Christmas," she said, and disappeared upstairs.

Nice kid. Lousy judge of character.

I got the tree up the chimney. Then, for

good measure, I took the log out of their fire. What would they need with a fire, anyway? It was only twenty below zero.

And then . . . I took all of the Whos' Christmas presents and trappings and anything else related to the holiday and flew them back to my hole in the wall.

Actually, the sleigh broke down halfway there and Max had to drag it up Mt. Crumpit. But it was worth it.

We reached the top just as dawn was breaking over Whoville. I pushed the sleigh until it was balanced right over the cliff.

"They're just waking up!" I told Max gleefully. "And I can just imagine what will happen next . . ."

I saw it all through my periscope. And it was a sight to behold.

Whos awoke all over Whoville and saw that Christmas had disappeared . . . and a great "Boo-Who" went up from a thousand throats.

They stumbled numbly into the streets and looked at one another. They all realized at the same time that this terrible calamity had happened to all of them. That someone had . . . absconded with Christmas.

Mayor May Who was one of the last on the scene. Actually, he slid onto the scene in his bed, which I had rigged (remember that booby trap I mentioned?) to come crashing out the window. And he was not a pretty sight without his girdle, in his hair curlers, wearing a chin strap . . .

It was glorious.

"Look what happened!" May Who blabbered, trying to save face. "Someone strapped this ridiculous thing to my face"—(I had done that, too!)—"and added thirty pounds to my hips and thighs!"

"I'd say more like forty-five," said Who Bris maliciously.

"Shut up," answered the mayor. "If you're looking to point the finger, the fiend who did this to me and to all of us . . . is up THERE!"

He pointed to the top of Mt. Crumpit.

I made a small bow of acknowledgment.

"You've got it all wrong!" said Cindy Lou, pushing to the front of the crowd. "It wasn't the Grinch who took the presents . . . it was Santa."

The Whos turned to her, astounded.

"I saw him," she went on. "He took our tree to fix it. He has a time-share at the South Pole . . . with Sasquatch."

There was a smattering of laughter in the crowd.

Gullible child. No one has time-shares anymore.

"Christmas is ruined!" moaned May Who.

Talk about getting everything you wanted for Christmas!

"I told you, invite the Grinch, destroy Christmas. But did anyone listen?" the mayor went on.

"I did," said Who Bris.

"Noooo," May Who went on, ignoring him. "You chose to listen to a six-year-old girl."

He turned to Cindy Lou. "Cindy Lou, I hope you're very proud of what you've done."

A small tear formed in Cindy Lou's left eye and began to travel down her cheek.

"Well, if she isn't . . . I am."

Astonished, Cindy Lou turned to see who had spoken.

It was her father.

Lou stepped between the mayor and his daughter.

"I'm glad the Grinch took our presents," he said stoutly.

There were puzzled murmurs from the crowd.

"Because that's not what Christmas is really all about . . . gifts and contests and fancy lights . . ." Lou turned to his wife. "Sorry, dear."

One or two Whos started to nod. Others listened.

"And I guess that's what Cindy Lou's been trying to tell everyone. And me! She was trying to tell me Christmas is about being together with our families and loved ones! And that's all. Everything else is . . . superfluous. And that means unnecessary.

"Doesn't it?" Lou turned to Cindy Lou.

Cindy Lou nodded. She wiped away the tear and started to smile.

"Merry Christmas, Dad," she said, giving Lou a big hug and kiss.

A smile started to spread over Lou's face, too.

"I don't need presents," Lou said happily. "What more could I want for Christmas than this?"

He turned to his wife again.

"Merry Christmas, Betty. I have absolutely nothing more to give you!"

Betty grinned.

"Merry Christmas, you hunk of burning

Who! I have absolutely nothing more to give *you.*"

They kissed.

Then Junie and Christina Who kissed Stu and Drew.

And then the rest of the crowd started kissing one another.

Ick!

"Merry Christmas, Mayor May Who," sniffled Who Bris. "I have nothing to give you except my eternal love."

"WHAT?" shouted May Who.

"I mean . . . respect. Merry Christmas . . . sir."

This was not going according to plan. What was happening in Whoville?

I could hear caroling! And sounds of good cheer!

Could it be that, despite my efforts, Christmas had come to Whoville, after all?

But it couldn't have! I had taken all the

presents . . . all the Christmas trees . . . all the Christmas feasts. They *couldn't* have Christmas! I had taken it all!

Or had I?

Maybe . . . Christmas wasn't about all the presents . . . or the trees . . . or the feasts.

Maybe it was about . . . a feeling . . . that you had inside . . .

"Oh, no! Max, help me!" I moaned. "I think . . . I think . . . I'm feeling!"

I could actually feel my heart grow three times as big in my chest.

It was terrifying . . . but sort of exhilarating.

"What's happening to me?" I cried. "I'm all toasty inside! Oh, Max! I love you!"

Max jumped into my arms and licked my face.

"That's enough, Max," I told him, flinging him to the ground. "Let's take this good cheer thing one step at a time, okay?"

Just then, I looked over and saw the

sled teetering on the edge of the cliff.

"Oh, no! The sled! The presents! Christmas will be ruined!"

Did I say that? Oh, my!

I raced to the sleigh and grabbed it by the rails. I struggled to hold it. It was slipping into the bottomless chasm below.

"Hi, Mr. Grinch!"

I looked up—and there was Cindy Lou, sitting on top of the sleigh!

"Cindy Lou!" I gasped. "What are you doing here?"

"I came to see you. No one should be alone on Christmas."

She smiled at me. *She smiled!*

And suddenly, I was filled with the strength of *ten* Whos.

I picked up that sled as if it were a candy cane and set it gently back on the mountain.

"You saved me!" said Cindy Lou.

"Saved you? *I* saved you?" I chortled. Then I stopped short.

"Well, yeah. I guess I did."

The next thing I knew, Cindy Lou and Max and I were sitting in the sleigh, whizzing down the mountain.

"How are you going to stop?" Cindy Lou wanted to know.

"Who cares?" I cried happily. "It's Christmas!"

Luckily, Martha May Whovier and Betty Lou Who spotted us at the same moment.

"Grinch?" breathed Martha May.

"Cindy Lou!" shouted Betty.

"Grab these lights!" said Betty, throwing the end of a long strand to Martha May. "We can stop them!"

They stretched a string of Christmas lights out between them across the road, catching the sleigh and stopping it just in time.

Officer Wholihan walked up to the sleigh, which, of course, was full of presents, and trees, and food.

"What do we have here?" he said. He was

clearly a master of the obvious.

"Ya got me, Officer," I admitted happily. "I did it. I am the Grinch who stole Christmas, and I'm sorry."

I put out my hands. "Cuff me and take me away. I'll go quietly."

But Wholihan just stood there.

"Don't you want to cuff me?" I begged. "Put me in a choke hold? How about pepper spray? I deserve it. I'm a loose cannon. I'm a live wire. I'm a threat to society!"

Mayor May Who stepped up.

"Well, you heard him, Officer," he said pompously. "He admitted it. I'd go with the pepper spray!"

"I heard him all right," said Wholihan. "He said he was sorry."

Mayor May Who's eyes bugged out in his head.

"But look what he did to our Christmas!" he shouted.

Wholihan walked around the sleigh.

"Everything seems to be here," he said calmly.

"He came into our houses! He made me wear curlers! BACK ME UP, PEOPLE!" May Who screamed.

Martha May Whovier, who had been scrounging around in the sleigh, came up with a small box.

"Merry Christmas, August May Who," she said. "I'm afraid I do have something for you . . . your ring back. Sorry."

She walked over to me and took my arm.

Mayor May Who looked a little stunned.

"It's all right. I'll be fine. She doesn't want to marry me. Okay. I have my hobbies. I'll be perfectly—"

He fainted.

The Who Biddies pushed through the crowd.

"There, there, dear," Clarinella said, picking up the limp May Who. "You come home with us."

"Whoticus! You've returned!" cried Rose, planting a kiss on the unresisting mayor's cheek.

"No, Rose," corrected Clarinella. She turned back to the mayor. "Come along. We've got a sweater that's the perfect size for you."

And they led the stunned mayor away.

"Wait!" shouted Who Bris, running after them. "Take me with you!"

I spent the next few hours putting Christmas back together again in Whoville. I gave back all the presents—even the ones the Who children had been dreaming of. I put up and decorated all their trees. I replaced the food, except for what I had eaten. (Well, you wouldn't want me to be *that* disgusting, would you?)

Finally, we were ready to relight the big town Christmas tree.

I screwed in the last bulb . . . and the whole town lit up.

It was . . . it was . . . beautiful.

"Merry Christmas, Mr. Grinch," said Cindy Lou, kissing me on the cheek.

She drew back in surprise.

"Your cheek! It's so—"

"Hairy?"

"No . . ."

"Dirty? Oily? Do I have a pimple?"

"No." Cindy Lou looked up at me and smiled. "It's so . . . warm!"

I looked down at Cindy Lou and smiled back. This time, she didn't fall into the postage-stamping machine.

"Merry Christmas, Cindy Lou," I said.

Then we all started singing a Christmas carol.

The Christmas celebration in Whoville that year was the greatest Christmas celebration any Who had ever seen.

It was more full of good cheer than any Christmas had ever been.

Fast friends were never faster and mortal enemies made up.

"I just wanted to tell you," Martha May told Betty, "I think . . . you had the nicer lights."

"And I should tell you," Betty responded, beaming, "I stole one of the headlights off your car."

We all stuffed ourselves full of roast beast and plum pudding and a really nice vintage Margaux.

And Martha May Whovier sat next to me throughout the whole Christmas feast.

"Grinchy, darling," she murmured as she poured me another drink, "I have a fabric that matches the fungus on your cave walls exactly!"

"What's that now?" I mumbled back.

"Well," Martha May said, "we're going to have to redecorate if we're doing all that entertaining. You know, starting tomorrow, we've got to get ready for Easter."

I blinked.

"EASTER???? I DESPISE EASTER!" I shouted. "I mean, Christmas is one thing, but Easter is the *worst!!!* Children all hopped up on mass quantities of chocolate. Women wearing bonnets . . . And those confounded bunnies! I had a bunny once. All he did was eat and poop and chew electrical wires. And when I tried to pet him, he bit me! Twelve rabies shots in the gut . . . Put that in your frilly bonnet! And then there's the egg painting . . . 'Look, Daddy . . . I put sparkles on this one. It's for you.' 'Thank you, my dear. That's the most beautiful sparkling DEAD CHICKEN EMBRYO I've ever seen!' NO! Easter is unacceptable. It's preposterous. It's rhinosterous! It's double-gabble-dardosterous . . .

"Out! Everybody out!"

I mean, a Grinch has to draw the line SOMEWHERE!